NANA
LOVES YOU MORE

To Grandma and Grandma,
GG and Nomma—the NANAs in my life

A Feiwel and Friends Book
An imprint of Macmillan Publishing Group, LLC
120 Broadway, New York, NY 10271 • mackids.com

Our books may be purchased in bulk for promotional, educational, or business use.
Please contact your local bookseller or the Macmillan Corporate and Premium Sales Department
at (800) 221-7945 ext. 5442 or by email at MacmillanSpecialMarkets@macmillan.com.

Library of Congress Cataloging-in-Publication Data is available.

First edition, 2022
Book design by Rich Deas and Miguel Ordóñez
Feiwel and Friends logo designed by Filomena Tuosto
Printed in China by RR Donnelley Asia Printing Solutions Ltd.,
Dongguan City, Guangdong Province

This special edition was printed for Kohl's, Inc. (for distribution on
behalf of Kohl's Cares, LLC, its wholly owned subsidiary) by Feiwel and Friends,
an imprint of Macmillan Publishing Group, LLC.

ISBN 978-1-250-82394-6 (hardcover)

ISBN 978-1-250-89841-8 (Kohl's Exclusive)

Kohl's, Inc.
Style: 98418
Factory Number: 123386
Production Date: 12/2022

1 3 5 7 9 10 8 6 4 2

Ages 3 and up

NANA
LOVES YOU MORE

JIMMY FALLON

ILLUSTRATED BY MIGUEL ORDÓÑEZ

FEIWEL AND FRIENDS
NEW YORK

NANA will read to you
and sing you to sleep.

And fill you with memories
that you'll always keep.

Forever from one past
one hundred and four,

You'll always love NANA,
but NANA loves YOU more.

More than the moon?
More than the stars?

More than all of the planets by far!

More than Paris and the Eiffel Tower?

More than cats with
SUPER cat powers.

More than rainbows?
More than dreams?

More than three scoops
of your favorite ice cream!

More than a bath overflowing with bubbles?

NANA will even love you when you get in trouble.

More than whales and more than cheese?

More than flowers
and rivers and trees.

More than candy
and things that are sweet?

More than anyone
you'll ever meet.

More than the biggest
of all birthday cakes?

I love you more than
any cake I could bake.

More than swimming in chocolaty fountains?

More than the feeling when you've climbed a huge mountain.

More than the horns
of a giant big band?

I hear my own music
when I'm holding your hand.

More than fireworks
that light up the skies?

More than the sunsets
and the sunrise.

More than gold or treasure or money?

You are my treasure.
You are my honey.

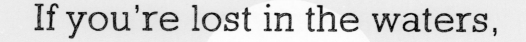

If you're lost in the waters,

I will lead you ashore.

I know you love NANA,

but **NANA** loves you more.